INDIANAPOLIS COLTS

BY JOSH ANDERSON

Stride
An Imprint of The Child's World®
childsworld.com

The Child's World
childsworld.com

Published by The Child's World®
800-599-READ • www.childsworld.com

Photography Credits
Cover: © Jonathan Daniel / Staff / Getty Images; page 1: © Africa Studio / Shutterstock; page 3: © Andy Lyons / Staff / Getty Images; page 5: © Joe Robbins / Stringer / Getty Images; page 6: © Tony Duffy / Staff / Getty Images; page 9: © Jonathan Daniel / Staff / Getty Images; page 10: © Michael Hickey / Stringer / Getty Images; page 11: © stevezmina1 / Getty Images; page 12: © Justin Casterline / Stringer / Getty Images; page 12: © Leon Halip / Stringer / Getty Images; page 13: © Michael Hickey / Stringer / Getty Images; page 13: © Jim McIsaac / Stringer / Getty Images; page 14: © Joe Robbins / Stringer / Getty Images; page 15: © Andy Lyons / Staff / Getty Images; page 16: © Harry How / Staff / Getty Images; page 16: © Wizardman / Wikimedia; page 17: © MALCOLM W. EMMONS/ZUMAPRESS / Newscom; page 17: © Joe Robbins / Stringer / Getty Images; page 18: © Cliff Welch/Icon SMI / Newscom; page 18: © Michael Conroy / Associated Press; page 19: © Donald Miralle / Staff / Getty Images; page 19: © Jonathan Daniel / Staff / Getty Images; page 20: © David Berding / Stringer / Getty Images; page 20: © Chris Unger / Stringer / Getty Images; page 21: © Jonathan Daniel / Staff / Getty Images; page 21: © Julio Aguilar / Stringer / Getty Images; page 22: © Andy Lyons / Staff / Getty Images; page 23: © Al Bello / Staff / Getty Images; page 23: © stevezmina1 / Getty Images; page 25: © AP / Associated Press; page 26: © Andy Lyons / Staff / Getty Images; page 29: © Streeter Lecka / Staff / Getty Images

ISBN Information
9781503857643 (Reinforced Library Binding)
9781503860513 (Portable Document Format)
9781503861879 (Online Multi-user eBook)
9781503863231 (Electronic Publication)

LCCN 2021952629

Printed in the United States of America

BRINGING THE WORLD TO YOUNG READERS 1968

TABLE OF CONTENTS

GO COLTS!

The Indianapolis Colts compete in the National Football **League's** (NFL's) American Football Conference (AFC). They play in the AFC South **division**, along with the Houston Texans, Jacksonville Jaguars, and Tennessee Titans. Fans in Indianapolis have seen a lot of success from their team. The Colts made the **playoffs** 18 times between 1995 and 2020 and won ten division titles. The **franchise** has been home to some of the best quarterbacks in NFL history. Let's learn more about the Colts.

AFC SOUTH DIVISION

Houston Texans

Indianapolis Colts

Jacksonville Jaguars

Tennessee Titans

THE COLTS WON 11 GAMES DURING THE 2020 SEASON AND FINISHED SECOND IN THE AFC SOUTH DIVISION.

BECOMING THE COLTS

The Colts began playing in 1953 in Baltimore, Maryland, as an NFL **expansion team**. They were named "Colts" because of Baltimore's history of horse racing. A colt is a young male horse. The team won two NFL Championships and one **Super Bowl** during their time in Baltimore. The Colts left Baltimore for Indianapolis, Indiana, before the 1984 season.

IT TOOK THE COLTS FOUR SEASONS TO EARN A TRIP TO THE PLAYOFFS AFTER RELOCATING FROM BALTIMORE TO INDIANAPOLIS.

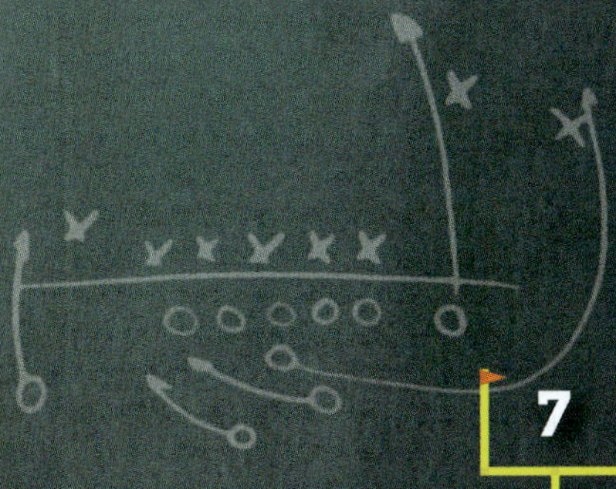

BY THE NUMBERS

The Colts have won the Super Bowl **TWO** times.

20 Colts enshrined in the Pro Football **Hall of Fame**

522 points for the Colts in 2004—a team record!

14 wins for the team in 2009

PEYTON MANNING LED THE COLTS TO THE PLAYOFFS DURING 11 OF HIS 13 SEASONS WITH THE TEAM.

PLAYER INTRODUCTIONS BEFORE GAMES AT LUCAS OIL STADIUM SOMETIMES INVOLVE SPECIAL EFFECTS AS THE TEAM RUNS THROUGH A GIANT HORSESHOE.

GAME DAY

For their entire time in Baltimore, the Colts played at Memorial **Stadium**. For the first 24 seasons after they moved to Indianapolis, the Colts played their home games at the RCA Dome. Then the team moved into Lucas Oil Stadium when it opened in 2008. The stadium, which features a **retractable roof**, hosted Super Bowl 47 between the New York Giants and the New England Patriots. On game days, Lucas Oil Stadium can hold about 67,000 fans.

We're Famous!

The NBC television show *Parks and Recreation* took place in the fictional city of Pawnee, Indiana. In one episode, to celebrate one of the character's upcoming wedding, his friends take him to Lucas Oil Stadium. At the stadium, the characters from the show meet team owner Jim Irsay and Colts legends Andrew Luck and Reggie Wayne.

UNIFORM

BLUE

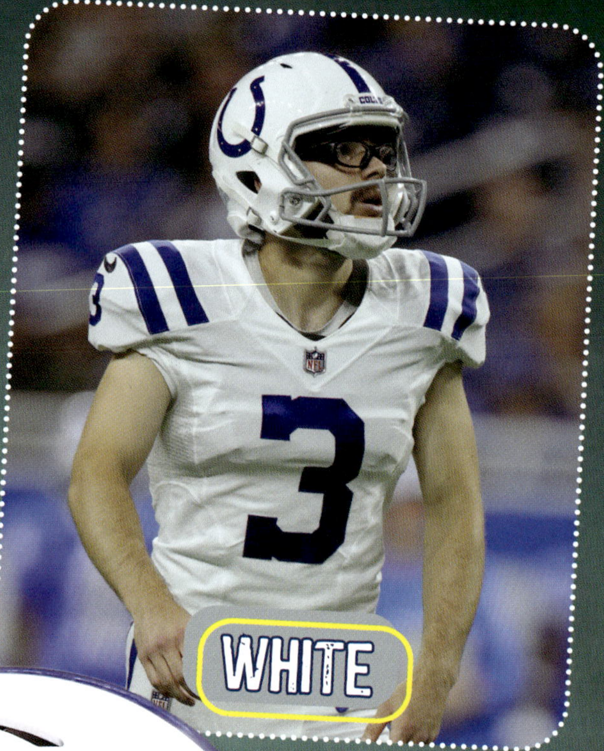

WHITE

Truly Weird

During a 2021 game against the Los Angeles Rams, the Colts scored a very unusual **touchdown**. The Rams lined up to punt the ball to the Colts in the fourth quarter. But instead of hiking the ball to their punter, the Rams' center snapped the ball off of another teammate. The ball bounced into the end zone. Ashton Dulin of the Colts dove on top of the ball, earning the Colts six points.

Alternate Jersey

Sometimes teams wear an alternate jersey that is different from their home and away jerseys. It might be a bright color or have a unique theme. In 2010, the team wore 1955 Baltimore Colts throwback uniforms. But the special threads proved unlucky. The Colts lost the game to the Philadelphia Eagles.

DONTE MONCRIEF PLAYED FOUR SEASONS FOR THE COLTS FROM 2014 UNTIL 2017.

TEAM SPIRIT

Every game at Lucas Oil Stadium begins with a Colts fan using a hammer to bang the anvil. Anvils are used to make horseshoes. The anvil is very large and made of iron, and the sound can be heard throughout the building. It's been a tradition before home games since 2017. Since 2006, the team's mascot, Blue, has been entertaining fans at Colts games. Blue is a giant blue horse who wears a jersey with the team's logo on the front. Blue was chosen in 2020 for induction to the Mascot Hall of Fame. The Colts Cheerleaders join Blue on the sidelines at every game.

BLUE

HEROES OF HISTORY

Marvin Harrison

Wide Receiver | 1996–2008

Harrison's 14,580 receiving yards place him ninth all-time in NFL history. He's also fifth all-time with 1,102 receptions and 128 touchdown catches. The eight-time Pro Bowler was part of the Colts team that won Super Bowl 41. Harrison is a member of the Pro Football Hall of Fame.

Gino Marchetti

Defensive End | 1953–1966

Marchetti was known as a top pass rusher of his era. He was selected for 11-straight **Pro Bowls** from 1954 to 1964. Marchetti was a key member of the Colts teams that won the NFL Championship in 1958 and 1959. He was elected to the Pro Football Hall of Fame in 1972.

Johnny Unitas

Quarterback | 1956–1972

Unitas led the Colts to two NFL Championships and a victory in Super Bowl 5. He led the league in passing yards four times. Unitas was a three-time winner of the **Most Valuable Player** (MVP) Award. The ten-time Pro Bowler is a member of the Pro Football Hall of Fame.

Reggie Wayne

Wide Receiver | 2001–2014

Wayne totaled 14,345 receiving yards in his career, which ranks tenth all-time. He also ranks tenth all-time with 1,070 receptions. Wayne was chosen for the Pro Bowl six times, and he helped lead the Colts to a Super Bowl victory after the 2006 season.

The Colts defeat the Dallas Cowboys 16–13 to win Super Bowl 5.

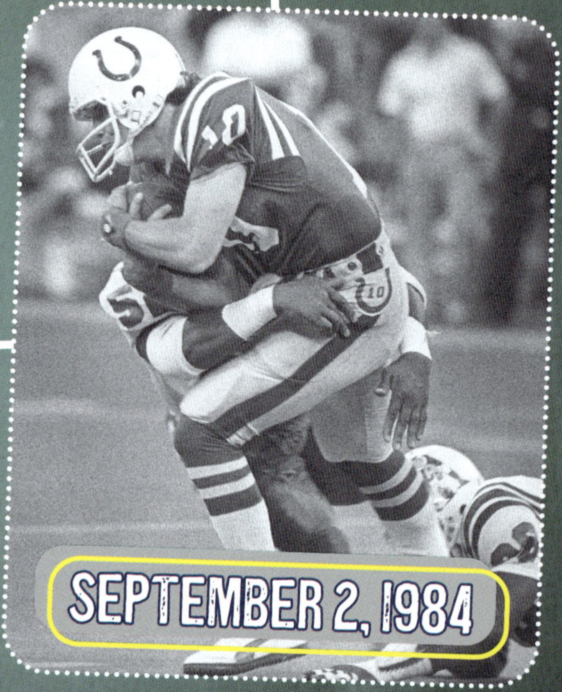

The Colts play their first-ever game in Indianapolis.

BIG DAYS

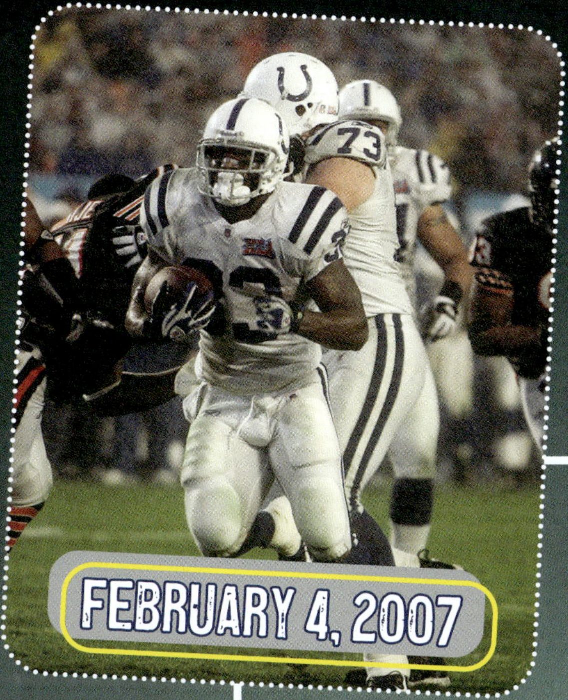

The Colts defeat the Chicago Bears 29–17 in Super Bowl 41.

A 30–17 victory over the Jets in the AFC Championship Game sends the Colts to Super Bowl 45.

MODERN-DAY MARVELS

DeForest Buckner

Defensive Tackle | Debut: 2020

Buckner joined the Colts in a trade in 2020. In 2020, he set a Colts single-season record for a defensive tackle with 9.5 **sacks**. In his first six seasons, Buckner totaled 389 combined tackles, 45 sacks, and five forced fumbles.

T. Y. Hilton

Wide Receiver | Debut: 2012

Hilton led the NFL with 1,448 receiving yards in 2016. He was selected for the Pro Bowl each year from 2014 to 2017. By the end of 2018, Hilton's 12 games with 150 or more yards receiving were the most in Colts history.

Darius Leonard

Linebacker | Debut: 2018

Leonard was a second-round draft pick for the Colts in 2018. He rewarded the team by winning Defensive Rookie of the Year after his first season. Leonard is the only player in NFL history with at least 300 tackles in his first 30 games.

Jonathan Taylor

Running Back | Debut: 2020

The Colts selected Taylor in the second round of the 2020 NFL Draft. He finished third in the NFL as a **rookie** with 1,169 rushing yards. Taylor led the NFL with 1,811 rushing yards and 18 rushing touchdowns in 2021. That year, he earned his first trip to the Pro Bowl.

PEYTON MANNING SET THE COLTS' SINGLE SEASON RECORD FOR PASSING TOUCHDOWNS WHEN HE THREW 49 OF THEM IN 2004.

THE GOAT

GREATEST OF ALL TIME

PEYTON MANNING

Manning ranks third all-time in passing yards (71,940) and passing touchdowns (539). He led the Colts to victory in Super Bowl 41 after the 2006 season. Manning was selected for 14 Pro Bowls, tied for the second-most of all-time. He also won the MVP Award five times in his career—more than any other player. Manning was elected to the Pro Football Hall of Fame in 2021.

FAN FAVORITE

Andrew Luck–Quarterback

2012–2018

Luck made the Pro Bowl in four of his six seasons before retiring at age 29. He led the league with 40 touchdown passes in 2014. After missing the 2017 season with an injury, Luck came back to win Comeback Player of the Year after the 2018 season.

THE BIG GAME

DECEMBER 28, 1958 – NFL CHAMPIONSHIP GAME

The 1958 NFL Championship Game is known by many as the "Greatest Game Ever Played." Led by quarterback Johnny Unitas, the Baltimore Colts played the New York Giants at Yankee Stadium in New York. With about two minutes left in the game, the Colts trailed 17–14. Starting at their own 14-yard line, Unitas led the Colts down the field and set up a game-tying field goal. In overtime, the Colts forced the Giants to punt before getting the ball at their own 20-yard line. The Colts again drove nearly the entire length of the field before Alan Ameche's rushing touchdown sealed a 23–17 victory.

ALAN AMECHE (RIGHT) CARRIED THE BALL INTO THE END ZONE FOR THE WINNING TOUCHDOWN IN THE 1958 NFL CHAMPIONSHIP GAME.

TONY DUNGY LED THE COLTS TO 85 REGULAR-SEASON VICTORIES.

AMAZING FEATS

4,761 Passing Yards

In 2014 by QUARTERBACK Andrew Luck

1,659 Rushing Yards

In 1988 by RUNNING BACK Eric Dickerson

16 Rushing Touchdowns

In 1964 for RUNNING BACK Lenny Moore

19.5 Sacks

In 2013 for DEFENSIVE END Robert Mathis

ALL-TIME BEST

PASSING YARDS

Peyton Manning
54,828

Johnny Unitas
39,768

Andrew Luck
23,671

RUSHING YARDS

Edgerrin James
9,226

Lydell Mitchell
5,487

Marshall Faulk
5,320

RECEIVING YARDS

Marvin Harrison
14,580

Reggie Wayne
14,345

T. Y. Hilton
9,691

SACKS*

Robert Mathis
123

Dwight Freeney
107.5

Ordell Braase
80

*unofficial before 1982

SCORING

Adam Vinatieri
1,515

Mike Vanderjagt
995

Dean Biasucci
783

INTERCEPTIONS

Bobby Boyd
57

Don Shinnick
37

Eugene Daniel
35

ADAM VINATIERI PLAYED 24 SEASONS IN THE NFL—14 OF THEM WITH THE COLTS.

GLOSSARY

division (dih-VIZSH-un): a group of teams within the NFL that play each other more frequently and compete for the best record

expansion team (ek-SPAN-shun TEEM): a new team added to the league

franchise (FRAN-chyz): a professional sports team

Hall of Fame (HAHL of FAYM): a museum in Canton, Ohio, that honors the best players in NFL history

league (LEEG): an organization of sports teams that compete against each other

Most Valuable Player (MOHST VALL-yuh-bul PLAY-uhr): a yearly award given to the top player in the NFL

playoffs (PLAY-ahfs): a series of games played after the regular season that decides which two teams play in the Super Bowl

Pro Bowl (PRO BOWL): the NFL's All-Star game where the best players in the league compete

retractable roof (ree-TRAK-tuh-buhl ROOF): a covering to a building that can be removed when necessary

rookie (RUH-kee): a player playing in his first season

sack (SAK): when a quarterback is tackled behind the line of scrimmage before he can throw the ball

stadium (STAY-dee-uhm): a building with a field and seats for fans where teams play

Super Bowl (SOO-puhr BOWL): the championship game of the NFL, played between the winners of the AFC and the NFC

touchdown (TUTCH-down): a play in which the ball is brought into the other team's end zone, resulting in six points

FIND OUT MORE

IN THE LIBRARY

Bulgar, Beth and Mark Bechtel. *My First Book of Football.* New York, NY: Time Inc. Books, 2015.

Jacobs, Greg. *The Everything Kids' Football Book, 7th Edition*. Avon, MA: Adams Media, 2021.

Sports Illustrated Kids. *The Greatest Football Teams of All Time*. New York, NY: Time Inc. Books, 2018.

Wyner, Zach. *Indianapolis Colts*. New York, NY: AV2 Books, 2020.

ON THE WEB

Visit our website for links about the Indianapolis Colts:
childsworld.com/links

Note to parents, teachers, and librarians: We routinely verify our web links to make sure they are safe and active sites. Encourage your readers to check them out!

INDEX

ABOUT THE AUTHOR

Josh Anderson has published over 50 books for children and young adults. His two boys are the greatest joys in his life. Hobbies include coaching his sons in youth basketball, no-holds-barred games of Apples to Apples, and taking long family walks. His favorite NFL team is a secret he'll never share!